Library and Information Centres
Red Doles Lane
Huddersfield, West Yorkshire
HD2 1YF
12/17

This book should be returned on or before the latest date stamped below.
Fines are charged if the item is late.

ou may renew this loan for a further period by phone, personal visit or at
vw.kirklees.gov.uk/libraries, provided that the book is not required by
ther reader.

NO MORE THAN THREE RENEWALS ARE PERMITTED

HOTEL FLAMINGO
CARNIVAL CAPER

ALEX MILWAY

Piccadilly
PRESS

First published in Great Britain in 2019 by
PICCADILLY PRESS
80–81 Wimpole St, London W1G 9RE
www.piccadillypress.co.uk

A CIP catalogue record for this book is available from the British Library.

ISBN: 978-1-84812-8071

also available as an ebook

1

Printed and bound in China

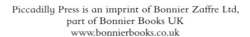

Piccadilly Press is an imprint of Bonnier Zaffre Ltd,
part of Bonnier Books UK
www.bonnierbooks.co.uk

For Katie

CAN YOU
FIND ME
IN THE STORY?

Port Whisker

Sea Dog
Pirate Tours

Zoozoo Theme Park

Tusks Cinema

Le Chat Shopping Mall

Dukduk Bowling

The Boulevard
Sports Arena

ANIMAL BOULEVARD

Hotel Flamingo

Lookout
Point

Sandy Dunes

Savannah Beach

Fort Rhino

Carnival Calling

Anna watched on as T. Bear and Stella decorated the front of Hotel Flamingo with giant feathery flamingos and shiny green palm leaves. Summer was officially over, but for the creatures of Animal Boulevard there was always something to celebrate. The highlight of autumn was the carnival, and as it was her first time Anna was keen to make a splash.

'More flamingos, do you think?' she said.

'I suppose you can never have too many!' said T. Bear.

The carnival was seen as the last hoorah before winter set in. It was a celebration of life, a huge parade, with exciting music and wonderfully exotic food. Everybody joined in, and revellers travelled from miles around to take part.

'All going well?' croaked Mrs Toadly, appearing at Anna's side. Mrs Toadly was a Carnival Director, and it was her job to ensure Animal Boulevard looked as wonderful as possible. At this time of year she never sat still, not even for a second. 'Your display is looking mighty fine!'

'Thank you!' said Anna. 'I thought we'd go for a pink theme.'

'I noticed,' said Mrs Toadly, laughing. 'I saw it from the other side of town.'

'Really?' said Anna, not sure if that was a good or bad thing. 'Too much, do you think?'

'There's no such thing as too much!' said Mrs Toadly. 'And that's why I'm here, to reward you for all this effort. You've made such a big impression on everyone

that I thought Hotel Flamingo should lead the parade.'

'Lead it?' said Anna. 'At the very front?'

'I take it you are entering a float?' asked Mrs Toadly. 'There's a competition for the best display each year.'

'What's a float?' asked Anna.

'It's an extravagant display on wheels,' replied Mrs Toadly. 'A truly terrific way to promote your hotel!'

Anna never missed a chance to sell Hotel Flamingo, but it would be a lot of work in such a short space of time.

'I'd have to ask the other staff to help,' she said.

'And don't forget, if your float wins, you'll get a Golden Palm!' said Mrs Toadly. 'It's a mighty fine honour.'

T. Bear climbed down from a ladder
with giant flamingo wings draped over
his shoulders.

'Carnival is in my
bones,' he said. 'I
know what to do.'

'So you'll take
part?' asked Mrs
Toadly.

T. Bear
whispered into
Anna's ear, 'It's

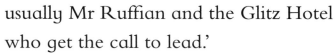

usually Mr Ruffian and the Glitz Hotel
who get the call to lead.'

Anna knew she couldn't refuse. 'We're
in!' she said.

'Wonderful!' exclaimed Mrs Toadly,
bouncing into the air. She carried on

down the road, leaping from foot to foot.
'The parade runs from the Opera House
to Boulevard's Cat's Paw sports arena.
Make it as bright and colourful as you
can imagine!' she cried.

'It'll be the biggest and brightest, filled
with dancers and music!' said T. Bear.

'Won't it, Miss Anna?'

'Yes, it will! We're going to win that Golden Palm!'

Anna and T. Bear walked inside, ideas filling both their heads.

'We only have a week to go,' said Anna, 'so call a staff meeting. We must make plans. I'll ask Ms Fragranti and her flamingos to join us!'

'Brilliant idea,' said T. Bear, clapping his paws together. He did a little dance. 'This is going to be the greatest carnival ever seen!'

2

Floating an Idea

Anna's office was filled with all her staff.

'We're entering the carnival float competition,' she said. 'We will have flamingo dancers, but I want your ideas for our display. It has to be impressive!'

'Who's going to be building this float thing?' asked Stella, raising an eyebrow.

Anna blushed. 'Ummm,' she mumbled,

'I was thinking we
could all . . . well
. . . help you?'
Stella laughed.
'It's fine,' she said.
'I'll add it to my list
of jobs. Besides, I'm
an old hand at carnival
floats. What did you have
in mind?'

'A huge robotic
flamingo that walks down
the street!' suggested T. Bear.

'And breathes fire!' added
Lemmy.

Stella looked uncertain.
'Yeah. How long have I got?'
she asked.

'We only have a week,' said Anna.

'I'm not saying it can't be done,' said Stella, 'but . . .'

'A magnificent, towering squid scone!' declared Madame Le Pig. 'We should celebrate our hotel's *pièce de résistance*!'

'Good thinking,' said Anna, keeping the chef on side. 'Let's keep these ideas coming, but also remember how long we have to make it.'

'You know,' said Stella, rubbing her chin, 'I actually do like T. Bear's idea.'

'Really?' said Anna. 'A giant flamingo?'

'I have my old work van that's doing nothing but gaining rust,' added Stella. 'I could probably make use of that.'

'Will it be fire-breathing?' asked Lemmy excitedly.

'Let's see what I can find lying around this place,' said Stella. 'You never know.'

Lemmy punched the air.

'We're going to the party!' said Eva happily.

•

As everyone got back to work, Anna scanned through the bookings and new arrivals for the day. New guests always proved a challenge and required special – or at least unique – treatment.

On the list were a pair of skunks and a flock of parrots, as well as a peculiar group booking, which had been doodled around in red pen. This could only be the work of one member of staff, she thought.

She called out to the front desk. 'Lemmy?'

'Yes?' he said, poking his head round the door.

'Who are the Nocturnal Animals, and why are there hearts drawn around them?' she asked. 'This is our official register of guests.'

Lemmy blushed. 'Sorry, miss. They're a rock band,' he said, a little embarrassed. 'The biggest band in the world . . . my favourite band . . .'

'The biggest band in the world? Staying here?!' exclaimed Anna.

'They're playing a massive gig at the Cat's Paw Arena after the carnival,' said Lemmy. 'Haven't you seen the posters? It's going to be huge!'

'Why didn't you mention this?'

'They wanted it to be kept secret.'

'But not from the hotel manager, surely?'

Lemmy's tail curled up and down. 'No,' he said sheepishly. 'Just from all the fans. We'd be overrun if anyone found out about them staying here.'

'I suppose that does make sense,' said Anna. 'So what time are the band arriving?'

'Not till after midnight,' he replied. 'To keep things hush-hush!'

'OK,' said Anna. 'I guess it's going to be a late one then.'

Lemmy rubbed his paws together excitedly. 'And I can't wait!'

3

Flock and Roll

T. Bear met the new guests, fresh from
a minibus.

'Welcome to Hotel Flamingo!' he said.
'Make yourselves at home.'

'Good morning!' said Anna cheerfully.
'Let me take your names, and we'll get
your keys ready.'

'Mrs Kunkworth,' said a skunk
tentatively. She clutched a novel in her

paws and played her claws nervously up and down its spine. 'Room for two. I booked it a month ago. I think it's all paid. Is it paid?'

'That's fine,' said Anna calmly. 'I have you here on the list.'

'You do?' said Mrs Kunkworth. 'Oh, that's a relief. I always worry I've got something wrong.'

'Yes, we do worry,' said Mr Kunkworth.

'You've nothing to worry about now,' said Anna. 'We'll look after you.'

'That's good,' said Mrs Kunkworth. 'We mostly sleep in the day as well. Is that in the notes?'

'Yes, it is,' said Anna. 'Your beds are ready and waiting. If you need any food, please let us know in advance.'

'Oh, we prepare our own food,' said Mrs Kunkworth, looking to her husband. 'We like to know what we're eating, don't we?'

'We do,' said Mr Kunkworth.

'Whatever makes you happy,' said Anna.

There was a sudden squawk as six excitable parrots crashed through the revolving doors. 'Sorry!' announced the

flock, jabbering to each other about who should go inside first.

Mr Kunkworth flushed bright pink as a terrifically stinky smell rose about him.

'Do you have our room key?' asked

Mrs Kunkworth hurriedly. 'I'm so dreadfully sorry. It always happens when he gets a fright.'

Anna covered her nose and attempted to smile. She handed over the room keys as Lemmy grabbed their bags.

'This way!' he garbled, struggling to breathe.

Meanwhile, the parrots bundled their way inside, chattering and cheering.

''Ello!' said the lead parrot with a wink. 'Mac Macaw here. A room for six, please.' He stopped moving, then his head tilted ominously. 'But what is that smell?' he asked, pretending to vomit. 'That's the strangest air freshener I ever smelled. Say, Lil, you get a whiff of that?!'

Another parrot pretended to faint and fell over. The other parrots giggled and squawked, and Lil opened her eyes and laughed.

'We've had a little accident,' said Anna apologetically.

'Little?' said Lil. 'I've smelled better stinks on the belly of a mouldy old sloth!'

'It'll pass soon,' said Anna. 'I hope.' She collected room keys for the birds and handed them over. 'Room 360,' she said, collecting some luggage. 'Just a short hop in the lift.'

'Woohoo! I'll be glad to get out of this smell,' said Mac, flapping a wing back and forth across his beak. 'Oh yeah – I almost forgot – did you get the note about beds?'

'Note?' asked Anna.

'You see, beds are great for flowers,' Mac said cheerfully, 'but what we need is a long branch – or a pole. We aren't fussy.'

'I'll get that sorted right away,' she said.

'Nice,' said Mac, smiling. 'Thanks.'

Anna returned to her desk. 'I think I'd better call Hilary,' she said, picking up the phone. 'Though what might get rid of that smell, I don't know.'

And there can be no more loud, sudden noises near Mr and Mrs Kunkworth, she thought.

•

Hilary set to work on the smell while Anna searched for Stella, eventually finding her scrabbling through the shed. She was tossing bits of wood, chunks of metal and anything that might be useful for the float out into the open.

'I know you've got a lot on,' said Anna, 'but I've got some guests needing a bit of help.'

'What's that then?' asked Stella,

bending her head and neck out of
the shed.

'We need a branch for six parrots,'
said Anna. 'Beds are no good for them.'

'It'll have to be strong to hold that
many,' said Stella, sucking in air. 'Won't
be easy.'

24

'I know,' said Anna. 'But we must have something.'

Stella nodded. 'I was doing some work downstairs yesterday and saw some leftover curtain rods,' she said.

'Will they be strong enough?' asked Anna.

'You tell me,' said Stella. 'Let me go and look.'

'Thank you, Stella,' Anna said, heading back to her office. She sighed. The week had only just begun, and it wasn't going to get any easier.

The Secret

Stella dragged Anna excitedly downstairs.

'So I pulled out the poles from behind the cupboard,' said Stella, 'which are perfect for the parrots, by the way – and found these doors.'

'Where do they lead?' asked Anna.

'No idea!' said Stella, shaking her head. 'Judging by how much the wallpaper has faded around them, I reckon they haven't been seen for at least fifty years.'

'Not even T. Bear would have been working here then,' said Anna.

The worn metal double doors were chained and locked with a rusty iron padlock. Anna tugged it to be sure it was locked. It was.

'In all the time I've been at Hotel Flamingo,' she said, 'these doors have been hiding right underneath my nose. If only we had a key!'

'We don't need a key,' said Stella, pulling some heavy-duty bolt cutters from her belt. 'Out the way – oh, and watch your eyes.'

With a grunt and a spot of brute strength Stella cut the chain clean in two. It clanked noisily to the floor. 'After you,' she said.

Anna teased open the doors, slightly
fearful of what lay beyond. The rusted
door hinges squealed horribly.

'I'll get some oil,' said Stella.

'No you won't!' ordered Anna. 'You'll
stay right here until we get the lights on.'

'Try this,' said Stella, switching on
her torch.

She passed it to Anna, who pointed it through the opening. She was almost too shocked for words.

The room was so vast that it dwarfed the lobby – it was almost as big as the whole of the ground floor put together. Anna couldn't make out much of the details in the gloom, but her heart started to sing.

'I don't believe it,' she said, dragging the beam from left to right. 'It's a ballroom!'

'Who'd have thought it?' said Stella. 'Right beneath our feet all that time!'

'Get the lights working,' pleaded Anna.

Stella found the light switches, and after a few minutes of testing the wiring and fiddling with fuses, the ballroom was

lit up in a dazzling golden glow. Anna's
eyes opened impossibly wide and sparkled
in the light.

With billowing chandeliers and faded
yet impeccably stylish wall decorations,
the ballroom was wide enough for a herd
of elephants to line-dance side by side,
and long enough for a hundred-strong
conga snake.

'Seeing this almost makes me want to
put on my dancing shoes,' said Stella.

'You like to dance?' asked Anna.

'Oh no. These hooves are made for
changing light bulbs, not the cha-cha-
cha!' said Stella. 'Still, I admit, it's quite
something.'

Anna walked to the end of the
ballroom and found a wide, ornate

staircase that wound upwards. 'Where
does this lead?' she asked.

'Only one way to find out,' said Stella.

They climbed up to find their
path blocked by a barricade of wood
and stone.

'Looks like we've something else to discover,' said Stella.

'Another door upstairs?' said Anna.

'You'd want a proper entrance for the guests in the lobby, wouldn't you?' said Stella.

'Of course you would,' said Anna, still amazed. 'Can we open it up?'

Stella rolled her eyes. 'Another thing for my list,' she said, laughing.

5

The Nocturnal Animals

The tour bus arrived in the dead of night, its lights sparkling in the falling rain. Autumn was rearing its blustery head earlier than usual, but T. Bear and Anna were prepared. They had umbrellas at the ready.

'Remember,' said Anna, 'they asked for secrecy!'

'Don't worry, miss,' said T. Bear, puffing out his chest to make himself bigger and more imposing. T. Bear could be quite the bodyguard when he needed to be.

The hotel was fully at sleep, but for two fruit bats enjoying a late-night mango cocktail in the Piano Lounge. Lemmy took them a bowl of dried apricot chips and walked back to the lobby, certain that they wouldn't bother them.

'I can't believe the band are here!' he said, unable to contain his excitement. 'Do you think they'll sign my tail?'

'I think we should be professional about their stay,' said Anna. 'Don't you?'

'Sorry,' muttered Lemmy. 'It's just too exciting.'

Under the cover of the umbrellas they ventured outside, and T. Bear opened the tour-bus door. 'Evening, all,' he said.

'Welcome to –'

A rather angry-looking honey badger trudged down the bus steps. His large-collared shirt was unbuttoned to his stomach, and a garish necklace hung low from his neck. He flashed a furious look at the sky.

'I hate rain,' he interrupted. 'Everything in place and ready for us?'

'Yes, sir,' said Anna.

'Better be,' he replied. He held out his paw to Anna. 'Mr Sweet. Manager of the band.'

'Ms Dupont,' said Anna. 'Manager of the hotel.'

The honey badger's handshake was firm to painful, and Anna was convinced his claws were purposely digging into her hand.

'Now, you listen good,' said Mr Sweet. 'And you pass these words on to your staff. You don't look at the band. You don't talk to the band. You don't ask for signatures or photos with the band. You got it?'

Lemmy's joy turned to sadness.

'Yes, sir,' said Anna.

'Good,' said Mr Sweet. 'Come on then.

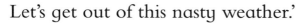

Let's get out of this nasty weather.'

Anna stepped back a little, lifting her umbrella high as the three band members left the tour bus. With slashed T-shirts, ripped trousers and boots up to their knees they absolutely looked the part. And although she tried not to look at them, she found it impossible not to peek. As did Lemmy. He whispered their names as they passed.

'That's Kool Bananas. He's a bushbaby and plays drums. And that's Anji Wax . . .'

Lemmy was so star-struck he found it hard to breathe, let alone speak.

'She's a wombat and plays bass. She never talks in interviews – she's too cool for that. And that's Suzi Suzi, a bat-eared fox. She's the singer and guitarist –'

Suddenly Mr Sweet grabbed Lemmy by the collar. 'Did you hear what I said about looking at the band?' he growled. 'Show them respect.'

Mr Sweet was even more terrifying than Madame Le Pig. Lemmy didn't know what to say or do. His tail fell

limply to the floor.

Thankfully T. Bear intervened. He placed his very firm paw on Mr Sweet's arm and removed it from his friend. 'Respect needs to be earned, Mr Sweet,' he said.

Anna could see that there would be trouble ahead.

'Everything should be as you need,' she said calmly. 'I'll show you to your rooms.'

Mr Sweet growled at T. Bear. 'The roadies will bring the kit in,' he said menacingly. 'Keep your paws off it.'

'My pleasure,' said T. Bear.

The band skulked their way across the lobby and into the lift.

'Fifth floor, Squeak,' said Anna.

'Right away,' he replied, looking at the floor.

'Nice hotel,' said Suzi Suzi as the lift started to move. 'I love the flamingo vibe.'

'Sure is,' said Kool Bananas. 'I could live here. Loads of space for drum kits.'

Anji Wax stood silently, her fringe hanging over her eyes.

Anna wondered why anyone would be *too cool* to speak.

The lift bell chimed and Anna stepped out. 'Here are your rooms,' she said, passing Mr Sweet their keys.

'We'll need room service,' he said. 'It's been a long ride, and we're hungry.'

'You want food? Now?' said Anna.

'We're nocturnal,' said Mr Sweet with a growl. 'I thought this place was a hotel! Don't you do night meals?'

If only Lemmy had let her know about the band sooner, thought Anna.

'Yes, sir,' she said. 'Of course. Just call the front desk.'

She stepped back into the lift, feeling grumpier by the second.

'Manners cost nothing, do they,

Squeak?' she said as the lift doors closed.

'No, miss,' said the mouse. 'Can I sign off for the day now, miss?'

'Absolutely,' said Anna. 'Thank you, Squeak.'

6

The Midnight Feast

Anna rested on the front desk, growing
sleepier by the minute. It was way past
her bedtime, and waiting for the phone to
ring was as bad as waiting behind a sloth
in the queue for the toilet.

The band's roadies started dragging
crates of instruments and concert gear
through the lobby, guided by Lemmy.
Anna called him over.

'You could have told me they were nocturnal animals!' she said.

'I thought it was obvious from their name,' said Lemmy with a shrug.

'But they need feeding, Lemmy. And there's no one to cook. Madame Le Pig will be fast asleep.'

An escaped snare drum rolled across the carpet and Lemmy ran after it.

'Sorry!' he said, making a hasty escape.

•

Anna was very nearly asleep when the phone finally rang.

'Reception!' she said, pulling the phone to her ear.

'It's Mr Sweet,' said the honey badger. 'I've got our room service order.'

'Fire away,' said Anna, her pen at the ready.

'A snow grass and ginger root smoothie,' he said. 'One termite tortilla. A bowl of honey chips – oh yeah, and a dragonfruit salad. Got that?'

'Yes, sir,' Anna said. 'I'll have it with you as soon as it's ready.'

She put the phone down and rubbed her eyes. It was time to wake up Madame Le Pig, and she was not going to like it one bit.

Anna crept downstairs to the chef's bedroom, which was a little further along the corridor from her own. Madame Le Pig slept as loudly as she shouted. Her rasping snore rattled the door handle.

After a brisk – if cautious – rap on the door, Anna waited nervously. The snoring stopped, but there was no reply. She knocked again, and then the floodgates opened.

'WHO IS THIS DISTURBING MY BEAUTY SLEEP?!' squealed Madame Le Pig through the door.

Anna cringed. 'It's me. Anna,' she said. 'The Nocturnal Animals have requested food.'

'At this hour?' blasted Le Pig.

'They're awake at night,' said Anna, 'so they eat at night.'

'I am not stupid!' declared Madame Le Pig. 'I know what nocturnal means.'

'Sorry, yes, Madame,' said Anna.

'But I,' continued Madame Le Pig, 'am not nocturnal! So go away!'

Anna so desperately wished she could

make the food herself. 'Please,' she said. 'They're really important VIP guests.'

Madame Le Pig's door creaked open. She was wearing bunny-rabbit slippers and unicorn-covered pyjamas. 'VIP guests?' she snorted. 'Who are these VIP guests?'

'It's a rock band called the Nocturnal –'

'THE NOCTURNAL ANIMALS!' squealed Madame Le Pig, cutting Anna short.

'That's right.'

Madame Le Pig hurried back into her room and threw on a dressing gown and her chef's hat.

'Why didn't you say?!'

'I did . . .'

'They are the biggest band in the world,' snorted Madame Le Pig as she raced down the corridor. 'And easily the best! Not even my food is good enough for them!'

Did she really just say that? thought Anna, running after her.

Madame Le Pig was nothing if not surprising.

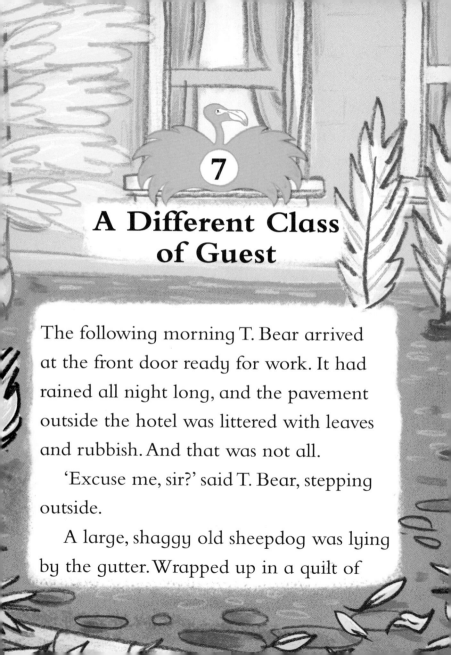

7

A Different Class of Guest

The following morning T. Bear arrived at the front door ready for work. It had rained all night long, and the pavement outside the hotel was littered with leaves and rubbish. And that was not all.

'Excuse me, sir?' said T. Bear, stepping outside.

A large, shaggy old sheepdog was lying by the gutter. Wrapped up in a quilt of

dirty newspapers, he looked asleep.
T. Bear nudged him gently and a sprinkling
of fleas burst from his damp, smelly fur.

The sheepdog grumbled a few
unrecognisable words.

'Sorry, sir,' said T. Bear. 'I don't think
you can lie here.'

'Why not?' growled the sheepdog.

'It's a busy road,' said T. Bear.

'Well, I ain't got nowhere
else to go cos of
this stupid

carnival,' replied the sheepdog and promptly rolled over.

'What's the carnival got to do with it?' asked T. Bear.

'They cleared us all off the streets,' said the sheepdog. 'They don't want us dirtying the place. So here I am.'

'Who doesn't want you on the streets?' asked T. Bear.

'Them Glitz folk,' grumbled the sheepdog.

'Hmph,' said T. Bear gruffly.

He plodded back inside the hotel to find Anna. 'We have a problem,' he said, scratching his ear.

Anna was barely awake after just a few hours' sleep. She sipped a cup of tea, hopeful that it might rouse her.

'Have the slug family left trails across the carpet again?' she asked.

'Not that I know of, miss,' he replied.

'Have the tarantulas spun another web across the corridor?'

'Not since yesterday,' said T. Bear.

'Oh,' said Anna. 'Then what is it?'

'We've an old sheepdog lying in our gutter,' said T. Bear. 'What should I do?'

'Is he in the way?' asked Anna.

'Very much so,' said T. Bear.

They walked to the front windows and Anna peered out over the road. 'Doesn't he have a home to go to?'

'I don't think so,' said T. Bear.

'Surely everyone has a home?'

T. Bear had seen a lot of life. He knew

how hard it could be at times. 'I don't think so, miss,' he said.

'You'd better invite him in then,' said Anna. 'We can't have him lying out there.'

'But . . .' said T. Bear, pausing. 'He . . . well . . . he smells of wet dog.'

'It can't be that bad, surely?'

'Maybe you should wait and see for yourself.'

•

It was true the sheepdog did smell of wet dog, thought Anna. But he had been asleep out in the rain.

'Excuse me, sir?' said Anna kindly. 'Don't you have somewhere to be?'

'Not any more,' growled the dog.

'Then would you like to come inside for some breakfast?'

All dogs are the same. They love food whether they have a home or not.

'Breakfast?' said the sheepdog, his ears lifting up.

'That's right,' said Anna. 'We have the best chef in town.'

The sheepdog sat upright, revealing his dense, shaggy fur. 'But I don't have money,' he said.

'That doesn't matter,' said Anna. 'What's your name?'

'Wilbur,' he replied with a smile.

'I'm Anna,' she said. 'In you come. Let's get you a cup of tea.'

8
Pamper Time

'I smell wet dog!' announced Hilary Hippo as she walked into the lobby.

Anna pointed to Wilbur, who was filling a small armchair while enjoying a cup of steaming-hot tea. His breakfast had vanished in seconds, and a tower of plates were piled up alongside him.

'It's Wilbur, our new guest,' said Anna.

Hilary sneezed as she caught sight of the sheepdog. Loose hairs and fleas were cascading from his legs on to the floor.

'I spent hours cleaning the carpet this morning!' said Hilary. 'It will need a thorough going-over again!'

'I'm sorry, Hilary,' said Anna. 'But everyone is welcome here, you know that.'

Hilary gave a firm nod. 'Don't let him move an inch,' she declared.

She raced from the lobby only to return a few minutes later carrying a smart bag.

'What's that?' asked Anna.

'My grooming kit,' she replied.

'Grooming?'

'I am much more than just a cleaner,' scoffed Hilary.

'But what if he doesn't want to be groomed?' asked Anna.

'I would never groom an animal without their permission first!' said Hilary. 'What do you take me for?'

She hurried over to Wilbur, sneezing on arrival. 'Mr Wilbur,' she said, 'when was the last time you visited a grooming parlour?'

'A what, miss?' asked Wilbur with a sniff.

'When were you last pampered?' asked Hilary. 'Groomed? Brushed? Washed?'

'Oh,' said Wilbur, tapping each claw on his left paw, 'now that would have to be four years ago, before I lost my job. Grooming's not cheap, not with all this fur.'

'Hotel Flamingo offers a pampering spa service for all new guests –'

'It does?' interrupted Anna.

Hilary furrowed her brow and continued. 'We can do manicures, pedicures and even flea treatment,' she said. 'All part of the service.'

Wilbur lifted off his tatty hat. A moth flew out. 'You can do all that for me?' he said, his ears lifting.

'All part of the service,' repeated Hilary.

'I think I may have died and gone to heaven,' said Wilbur.

'No, it's just Hotel Flamingo,' said Anna happily.

'We can't just let Wilbur stay here forever,' said Lemmy. 'We're fully booked up and, besides, our other guests might get annoyed that they've paid and he hasn't.'

Anna scratched her head. Of course, Lemmy was correct, but she really wanted to do the right thing. If only she knew what that was.

'It doesn't seem fair to send him back out on to the street,' she said.

'Try talking to him,' said T. Bear. 'There might be some way we can help.'

When Anna found Wilbur he was sitting in the Piano Lounge, resting his weary bones in one of the fancy armchairs. He was almost unrecognisable. His freshly cleaned fur was silky smooth

and ballooned around his head and
shoulders like a pompom.

'Is that you, Wilbur?' she asked.

'Yes, Miss Anna!' he said, smiling.

'Is there anything we can do to help
you?' she asked.

'You've already done enough, miss,' he said happily.

Anna wasn't so sure. 'Do you have a job to go to?' she asked.

'I did. I was in the army,' said Wilbur. He flexed his arm muscles. 'I'm strong, good at reading maps, and I can polish shoes to within an inch of their lives —'

He lifted his feet, waving around his sweet-smelling fur, but he seemed to have forgotten he wasn't wearing any shoes.

'But they don't want you once you get old.'

'And you couldn't get another job?' asked Anna.

'You can't get a new job without a home, and you can't get a new home without a job,' said Wilbur.

'I can see that makes life very complicated,' said Anna.

'It does, miss,' said Wilbur.

Anna sighed. 'We don't have any job vacancies,' she said sadly, 'or else you could work here.'

Wilbur shook his head and his fluffy hair wobbled about him. 'You've done plenty enough already,' he said.

Yet despite Wilbur's insistence, Anna wanted to do more. Perhaps there was something she could help with.

'We have empty staff bedrooms downstairs,' said Anna. 'They're not pretty, but you can use one of those until you find a new job.'

'No, no,' said Wilbur, 'that's too much.'

'I insist,' said Anna. 'It's a chance to put things right. It'll be up to you to make the most of it.'

'Do you really mean it?' asked Wilbur.

'I do,' said Anna. 'You said yourself, if you have a home, you can get a job. It's one part of the problem solved.'

Wilbur howled in happiness. 'I won't forget this, miss!' he said.

9

The Riotous Rehearsal

Anna was lying in bed when a loud knocking broke her sleep.

'Miss Anna,' said Lemmy, 'I'm so sorry, but I could do with some help.'

It wasn't like Lemmy to bother her at night. Anna rubbed her eyes, threw on her dressing gown and opened the door. 'What's wrong?' she asked.

'It's the band, miss,' he said. 'They're rehearsing!'

'What time is it?'

'Three in the morning,' said Lemmy. 'They've woken up nearly four floors. I've got two sad llamas, three honking baby geese and Mrs Turpington is in tears!'

'That's the last thing we need!' said
Anna, steeling herself. 'Right! Let's go and
have a word.'

Anna walked into the lobby and
could hear the thumping of drums and
the screeching of wild, distorted guitars
coming from the upper floors.

'I thought they wanted to keep their stay a secret?' said Anna. 'Everyone's going to know about them after this.'

Eva was consoling Mrs Turpington with a nice dandelion tea.

The ageing tortoise shook her head. 'Is this what they call music these days?' she said to Anna. 'You can't dance to this!'

'I'm sorry,' said Anna. 'It'll be quiet soon. I'll see to it.'

She took a deep breath and rode the lift to the fifth floor. Bleary-eyed guests poked their heads out of their doors as she passed. The music pounding out of the band's room was loud, angry, yet quite incredible, and with her fist firmly clenched she banged on the door.

'Can you turn it down, please?' shouted Anna.

The music continued and she banged again. 'Mr Sweet, will you open the door?'

A second or two passed before the music cut out. Anna's heart started to race. The door opened, and Mr Sweet's snarling face appeared before her.

'What?' he snapped.

'You cannot play music at this time of night,' said Anna. 'You've woken all our guests up.'

'We rehearse at night,' snarled Mr Sweet. 'That's when we're awake. Deal with it.'

He slammed the door. The music started again.

Anna stood silently for a moment, allowing her anger a chance to come off the boil. Nobody, not even a terrifying honey badger, could talk to her like that and get away with it.

She banged at the door once more. The music stopped and again Mr Sweet opened the door. 'What is it this time?' he snarled.

Faced with the terrifying creature her voice seemed to stop working. She coughed and forced out the words, 'In my office, now!'

Mr Sweet laughed. 'Are you threatening me, miss?' He bared his sharp teeth.

'In my office, now,' repeated Anna, finding her strength. 'I will not be spoken to like this in my hotel.'

And with that she turned and ventured back downstairs. Her heart was pounding, but she was feeling stronger for confronting Mr Sweet.

By the time Anna had reached the office, most of the staff were awake and placating upset guests. Even Jojo, who was better equipped to deal with swimmers than sad skunks, was doing her best to calm everyone down.

T. Bear was at the front desk, looking ready for action. 'Want me to deal with Mr Sweet, miss?' he asked, rubbing his paws together. 'I don't mind.'

'I think I have things under control,'

said Anna, 'but I'd love to have you as back-up!'

'Always, miss,' said T. Bear.

When Mr Sweet arrived Anna was sitting at her desk with T. Bear looming tall behind her.

'How dare you talk to me like that!' barked Mr Sweet, his claws pointing menacingly at Anna. 'You do realise how powerful I am?'

'Sir,' said Anna, 'you can act as strong and mean as you like, but this is my hotel. I deserve respect. As do all our other guests.'

'I manage the biggest band in the world,' he replied. 'You manage this pokey hotel. I should take my stars elsewhere.'

'You could try, but there will be no

spare rooms available at the Glitz,' said Anna. 'Not in carnival week.'

Mr Sweet seemed taken aback. Anna wondered if he wasn't used to having people question him. There was a knock on the office door. It opened and Suzi Suzi walked in, her guitar strapped over her back.

'Hey, man,' she said calmly to Mr Sweet. 'What's all this fuss?'

'Stay out of this,' said Mr Sweet. 'I've got it under control. This little hotel thinks it can mess us about.'

'No way, man,' said Suzi. 'That's not the way I see it. That lemur dude, he's just been telling me we woke the whole place up? Who wants that on their mind, man? We can practise somewhere else.'

Mr Sweet growled angrily. 'That lemur spoke to you?' he said.

'Yeah, dude,' said Suzi.

Mr Sweet turned to Anna. 'I told you there was no speaking to my band!'

'No wonder everyone's treating us weird, man,' said Suzi. 'Dude, chill out.'

'You know I could ruin you in a heartbeat!' Mr Sweet barked in rage. He stomped out of the room, leaving Suzi with Anna and T. Bear.

'That guy's out of order,' said Suzi. 'Hey, I'm sorry.'

Anna smiled, happy that Suzi was actually a nice fox. And in that moment Anna had a brilliant idea.

'I've got the perfect practice room, if that's what you want?' she said. 'And it's so far from the guests you won't bother a soul.'

'Yeah, man,' she said, nodding in a leisurely way. 'That would be awesome!'

'Mr Sweet won't mind?' asked Anna.

'He won't have a choice,' said Suzi. 'I've had enough of his negative energy anyway.'

'OK then,' said Anna.

Anna asked T. Bear to help the band move all their equipment into the ballroom, and she walked out into the lobby to find Lemmy totally entranced.

His cheeks were pink.

'Sh-she spoke to me,' he stuttered, staring off into space. 'Suzi Suzi spoke to me . . .'

10

The Bust-up

T. Bear waited in the ballroom as
the band tuned their instruments and
tightened their drum skins. Anji Wax
looped her bass guitar over her back
and sat back in a stink. T. Bear could
tell she was feeling down. Something
wasn't right within the band.

'Can I get you anything?' asked
T. Bear, trying to be helpful.

Anji shook her head, her sharp fringe wobbling across her face.

'Right!' shouted Mr Sweet, marching into the ballroom. 'Band meeting, now!'

'Dude,' said Suzi Suzi, 'we need to practise.'

'Do as I tell you,' threatened Mr Sweet. 'I am your manager!'

T. Bear shrank back against the ballroom wall so as not to be seen. There were very few people T. Bear didn't like, but he'd quickly realised Mr Sweet was one of them.

Suzi put her guitar down and crossed her arms. 'No,' she said. 'You're not the boss of me.'

Kool Bananas hammered his sticks on to a tom-tom. 'Nor me,' he said.

'I think you'll find I am,' growled Mr Sweet. 'Without me you're nothing.'

Kool leant forward, pointing his sticks at Mr Sweet. 'Without us *you're* nothing,' he said.

'Is that so?' said Mr Sweet. 'And what have *you* got to say about this, Anji?'

Anji snarled and threw her bass guitar to the floor.

'Like I thought,' said Mr Sweet. 'Nothing. So this is it then?'

'If that's how you want it, dude,' said Suzi. 'You've got a bad thing going on. It's bringing me – heck, it's bringing all of us – down.'

An angry Honey Badger is a terrifying

sight. Mr Sweet looked as though he was about to explode.

'Then we are done,' he snarled. 'And so is the band. And I'm taking the roadies with me. Good luck being a bunch of nothings for the rest of your miserable lives.'

Mr Sweet powered out of the ballroom, throwing a chair against a wall as he went.

T. Bear stepped out of the shadows.

'Sorry you had to see that, dude,' said Suzi. 'He is just one big bad vibe.'

'I've seen his type before,' said T. Bear, knowing he wasn't much different to Mr Ruffian of the Glitz. 'You're better off without him.'

Anji Wax nodded in agreement and

T. Bear was certain he caught a glimpse of a smile on her face. She picked up her bass guitar and checked it over.

'I hope so, dude,' said Suzi. 'This is the biggest gig of our lives coming up. I guess we'll have to wait and see, yeah?'

Kool Bananas tapped a two-four beat on his drum, and just like magic the band powered up and blasted out the most ferocious, loud and brilliant tune T. Bear had ever heard.

11
Demolition Day

The next day, Anna battled to keep her eyes open. 'All these night shifts are taking their toll,' she said.

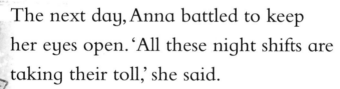

Lemmy was used to working the front desk at night, so he was also used to feeling tired.

'Power naps, that's how I cope,' he said. He pulled his hat slightly over his eyes and leant forward on the desk.

'Like this. No one ever knows.'

Anna smiled knowingly.

'Quite brilliant,' she replied.

The lobby was bustling with guests, but everyone seemed quiet and tired after being woken during the night. To apologise Anna had decided that all teas and coffees would be free for the day. That met with some cheer, particularly from Mrs and Mr Kunkworth, who

 were enjoying an early-morning nightcap before bed.

'Morning,' squawked Mac Macaw, dancing from

one leg to the other. 'Any chance of another coffee?'

Anna wondered if he'd already had a few, judging by how fidgety he was. Still, *the customer is always right*, she thought.

'I'll get you one now,' she said.

As she left the desk she was halted by the ominous sound of banging on the wall behind her.

'Wow!' said Mac. 'You've got some big woodpeckers staying here.'

THUD

THUD

'We don't have any woodpeckers staying here,' she said.

Lemmy had set off to investigate. He touched the walls, moving along as he tried to find the source of the noise. The banging continued, and he held his paw to a patch of wall near a bookcase. It shook with each thump.

'The noise is coming from behind here,' he said.

'What is it?' asked Anna.

'Giant moles?' said Mac excitedly.

'It's getting stronger!' said Lemmy, stepping away.

'And louder,' said Anna.

A rip suddenly shot through the wallpaper from floor to ceiling.

'Get back!' cried Anna.

Lemmy screamed and leapt backwards as lumps of brick and plaster fell from the wall. A dark and dusty hole appeared.

The banging stopped, and Mac clutched Anna's arm with fear. Lemmy looked at Anna, Anna looked at Mac, then they all stared back at the dusty hole.

Stella's head poked through. 'Morning!' she said, blinking in the light.

Mac howled with laughter while Anna breathed a huge sigh of relief.

'What have you done to the wall?' asked Lemmy.

'It's not a wall; it's a doorway,' said Stella. 'And that's the first item ticked off my list. Watch out!'

She disappeared again, only for more of the wall to crumble and tumble out into the lobby. Before long there was a proper doorway. It was dirty, and needed a bit of tidying, but the once glamorous entrance to the ballroom was now open.

'How's that?' Stella asked.

'Brilliant, though Hilary won't be happy with the mess,' said Anna.

'No pain, no gain,' said Stella.

Mac's wing crept over his beak. 'Oh no,' he said.

'What now?' said Anna.

'The smell's back,' he said.

Anna turned to see Mrs Kunkworth leading her husband out of the lobby. The shock of the wall disappearing had been too much for him.

'Hilary!' shouted Anna. 'I need you!'

12

The Night Shift

Anna spent the rest of the day in a daze, trying to be helpful, but not getting very far. She watched happily as Stella fixed the ballroom doorframe in the lobby and hung new glass doors.

'Next time, make a mess tidily!' said Hilary, distinctly unimpressed at having to vacuum the carpet again.

But by the time they had finished, the

lobby looked as good as new.

'It's like the hotel was always missing it, and yet I never knew!' said Anna.

'Another room for me to clean,' grumbled Hilary.

Anna hadn't considered the extra workload for Hilary. 'Yes. Sorry,' she said. 'I'll help you with that.'

'As long as you dust properly,' said Hilary.

'How hard can it be?' teased Anna with a smile.

'Cleaning is not a laughing matter,' said Hilary.

The day passed without any

further excitement. Anna followed Hilary's directions, and by the late evening the ballroom was looking fabulously spick and span. But once most creatures had gone to bed Anna realised she was too tired to stay up to cater for her nocturnal guests.

'Go to bed, miss,' said Lemmy, recharged after a power nap. He could see she was struggling. 'I've got the night shift covered. All meals have been prepared, and they're ready for the guests.'

'Thanks, Lemmy,' said Anna, drifting downstairs as her eyelids threatened to shut. 'Any trouble from Mr Sweet, come and get me.'

'I think he's long gone, miss,' said T. Bear, who was also heading off to bed.

'Really?' said Anna.

'The band had a big bust-up last night,' he replied.

'Well, I can't say I'm sad about seeing the back of Mr Sweet,' said Anna. 'He was a nasty piece of work.'

'That honey badger put Mr Ruffian in the shade,' said T. Bear.

Anna turned to Lemmy. 'Looks like it might be a quiet one,' she said.

'Exactly how I like it!' he replied.

•

As Lemmy tidied some papers on a table in the lobby the lift bell chimed. Kool Bananas walked out, rattling his drumsticks against a tall vase – rat-a-tat-a-tat!

'Goodnight!' said Lemmy. 'Or is it good morning for you?'

'Hey, Lem!' said Kool. 'Any chance of some food?'

'You bet!' said Lemmy, trying to sound relaxed. 'I'll get some now. Still no sign of your manager?'

'He's vanished,' said Kool, clacking his sticks above his head happily.

'But what about your gig?' asked Lemmy.

'We don't need him,' said Kool. 'You'll be coming, right? I'll get you in on the guest list.'

Lemmy felt the tummy rumblings of being star-struck again. 'You'd do that for me?'

'No trouble,' said Kool, drumming lightly on Lemmy's shoulders.

They went into the restaurant and found Wilbur asleep at one of the tables.

The sheepdog was still struggling to get used to having a roof over his head.

'What's the deal with him?' asked Kool.

'I love his hair. Think I could rock that look?'

'That's Wilbur,' said Lemmy. 'He's not had a home for years, so he tends to forget that he can go to bed.'

'I know how that feels,' said Kool. 'We've been on the road non-stop for two years. I don't even know where I live any more.'

Lemmy went to the sheepdog and rubbed his shoulder, gently waking him up. 'It's getting late, sir,' said Lemmy.

'Is it?' said Wilbur, yawning. 'Day and night, ain't much different to me.'

'Hey!' said Kool. 'You're a nocturnal animal, like us!'

'I s'pose I am,' said the sheepdog.

'And great hair,' said Kool.

'You like it?' said Wilbur.

'Yeah, it's massive!'

Wilbur smiled and held out his paw.
'Nice to meet you,' he said.

Wilbur was at least five times the size
of the bushbaby, but the two animals
shook paws.

'If you're about later,' said Kool, 'we're practising in the ballroom. Stop by.'

'Thanks,' said Wilbur. 'I will.'

Lemmy's eyes and mouth opened wide. There was nothing he'd like more than to watch the band play.

'Oh, Lem,' said Kool. 'You too! You're always welcome.'

Kool slipped his sticks in his pocket and sat at a table. 'Now for some food, yeah?' he said, smiling.

'Right away!' said Lemmy.

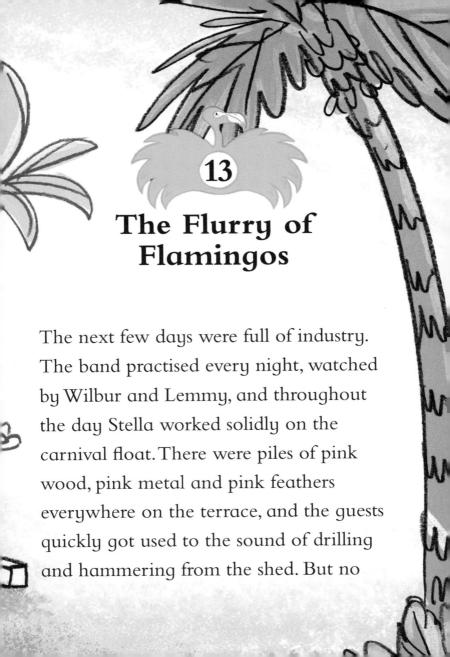

13

The Flurry of Flamingos

The next few days were full of industry. The band practised every night, watched by Wilbur and Lemmy, and throughout the day Stella worked solidly on the carnival float. There were piles of pink wood, pink metal and pink feathers everywhere on the terrace, and the guests quickly got used to the sound of drilling and hammering from the shed. But no one – not even Anna – was allowed to see what she was doing.

'Can I have a look?' asked Anna.

'I want it to be a surprise!' said Stella, slamming the shed door.

Anna crossed the terrace and watched Jojo dredge the pool for fallen leaves with the help of her pups. Despite the turn in seasons, the pool was still in great demand. Furry animals, as well as those with thick, blubbery skin, seemed very happy in the cooler temperatures.

As Anna ventured into the lobby she was cheered by the arrival of Ms Fragranti, the wildly theatrical flamingo.

'Darling!' Ms Fragranti cried, swooping into the hotel lobby, followed by her dance students. 'We are here!'

Anna skipped
up and down. 'So nice to
see you again!' she said.

'No flamingo needs to be asked twice
to join the carnival, darling!' said Ms
Fragranti.

Anna laughed. It was always
wonderful to have Ms Fragranti stay. 'Did
you have a good flight?' she asked.

'The winds blew us along at almost twice our normal speed!' she declared. 'I fear a storm is brewing. But the show must go on, whatever the weather!'

'It must!' agreed Anna.

'And is your costume ready?' asked the flamingo. 'I take it you are wearing more than that?'

'I hadn't thought about a costume,' said Anna.

Ms Fragranti tutted. 'Darling,' she said, 'if you're leading the carnival, you must BE the carnival. Bright colours, feathers, outrageous headgear! You must wear the brightest outfit you can find!'

Anna looked herself up and down, unsure. 'Maybe a big hat?' she said.

'Oh, please, darling! At the very least!' said Ms Fragranti. She gave Anna a wonderfully big smile.

'What?' said Anna, noticing a naughty twinkle in the flamingo's eye.

'I have packed for this very problem,' said Ms Fragranti, throwing her wings up into the air. 'For we have brought the carnival with us!'

•

'Is it not a bit much?' said Anna.

Anna was clothed in a magnificently bright, feathered outfit, with a headdress to match. So too was T. Bear and Lemmy. Ms Fragranti had prepared enough costumes for everyone.

'It's certainly a change from our uniform,' said T. Bear.

'I love it!' said Lemmy, flapping his new wings.

Ms Fragranti handed Lemmy a pair of maracas, and passed T. Bear a giant bass drum to strap on to his chest.

'I take it you can keep a beat?' said Ms Fragranti.

T. Bear's smile widened to fill his face. He pulled the drum straps over his shoulders then started to bang a rhythm.

'You bet,' he growled, wiggling his body to the groove.

'Then I think you are ready!' announced Ms Fragranti.

14

The Emergency Meeting

On the morning of the carnival, Anna received a phone call from Mrs Toadly, the carnival organiser. There was a meeting of the utmost importance and she had to attend. She left the hotel in Lemmy's capable hands, and set off to the Artists' Quarter.

Anna had never been to that side of town before, and in a colourful office tucked away off an ancient cobbled street she sat awaiting Mrs Toadly's arrival. There was barely any room to breathe inside, as everyone who was entering a float was present, including Mr Ruffian, owner of the Glitz. He didn't look very happy, thought Anna. But then, when did he ever?

Eventually Mrs Toadly skipped into the room, but without her usual broad smile.

'It would seem,' she said, 'that there is a mighty fine storm circling a few hundred miles off the coast. It may hit us this afternoon or it may not, but I fear we must cancel the carnival.'

'Ridiculous,' snapped Mr Ruffian. 'We never have storms here. This is the Sunset Isle after all!'

'The weather report was very sure,' said Mrs Toadly. 'Storm of the century, they said.'

'Weather reports are always wrong,' said Mr Ruffian. 'Besides, my hotel is booked full of guests! They're here because of the carnival.'

'As is mine,' said Anna.

Mr Ruffian growled at Anna under furrowed brows. He was still incredibly angry about Hotel Flamingo's success. He stood up and towered over Mrs Toadly. 'You cannot cancel the carnival!' he said, bearing down on her.

'We have to think of safety,' said Mrs Toadly.

'We have to think of all my unhappy hotel guests!' he replied in a bullying tone. 'Animal Boulevard would be a laughing stock. The carnival is the highlight of the year.'

Mrs Toadly fell silent. The other animals in the room mumbled with discontent.

'You cannot cancel the carnival,' repeated Mr Ruffian. 'It would be a disaster for us all!'

With a very loud, awkward gulp, Mrs Toadly finally spoke. 'If everyone's in agreement, then so am I,' she said. 'Everyone?'

'Will it really be dangerous?' asked Anna.

'WE DON'T GET DANGEROUS STORMS HERE,' growled Mr Ruffian. 'What would you know?'

He marched to the door. 'The carnival is on,' he said, stepping outside. 'And that's the last I'll hear of it.'

•

'Miss Anna!' said Lemmy as she walked into the hotel. He sounded quite distraught. 'Look at this!'

He held a poster for the carnival concert, but the Nocturnal Animals were no longer on the bill. Another band had taken their place.

'Who are the Sugar Bunnies?' asked Anna.

'They're rubbish,' said Lemmy. He hunched sadly over the front desk. 'I can't believe it. I was going to be on the guest list!'

'I'm sure it's all a big mistake,' said Anna. 'But I think I should go and tell the band.'

She knocked on the door to their room, and Suzi Suzi answered.

'Sorry to wake you,' said Anna.

'You didn't,' said Suzi. 'We stay up late. A chance to chill out after practice.'

Anna passed her the concert poster. 'Have you seen this?' she asked.

'Wow,' said Suzi in disbelief.

She walked into her room, beckoning Anna to follow. The room was tidy and well kept, and not at all how Anna thought a rock band would live.

'The dude's cancelled the gig,' said Suzi to Anji and Kool.

'And look who's playing now,' said Kool. 'The Sugar Bunnies? They're the worst.'

Anji sighed, and her broad shoulders slumped down. For the first time since staying with them Anna was surprised to see her fringe clipped back to reveal her beautiful dark black eyes.

'You've heard of them?' asked Anna.

Anji nodded.

Kool slammed his sticks on to a coffee table. 'They're Mr Sweet's other band,' he said.

'That now makes sense,' said Anna. 'So what will you do?'

'I guess we should pack up and leave,' said Suzi.

'But where will you go?' asked Anna.

'Home?' said Kool. 'I mean, it's been a while.'

'Stay here for the carnival,' said Anna. 'Sleep well, and then see how you feel later.'

'Are you cool with that?' asked Suzi.

'Of course I am,' said Anna. 'I know Lemmy's loved having you here. As have I.'

'You know,' said Kool, 'this hotel rocks.'

'I probably should go and get ready for the carnival now,' said Anna. 'Get some rest, and we'll catch up tonight.'

'Sure,' said Suzi.

Anna left and went to find her costume. What had once seemed so exciting now left a bad taste in her mouth. Still, as Ms Fragranti said, the show must go on.

15

The Carnival

Anna kicked her heels as she waited outside the hotel with Ms Fragranti and her students. A constant stream of carnival-goers made their way up Animal Boulevard. There were animals of all shapes and sizes dressed in outrageous costumes, and Anna was desperate to get going.

'It's taking forever!' she said impatiently.

'Don't you just love this feeling?' declared Ms Fragranti. 'It is the same thrill as seeing a stage for the first time, or hearing the first cry of *encore*!'

With a 'pish' and a 'puff', and a cheerfully loud 'SQUAWK!', a gigantic

pink flamingo trundled out from behind the hotel, its long neck and glorious smiling head leading the way.

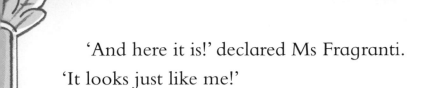

'And here it is!' declared Ms Fragranti. 'It looks just like me!'

'It's a flamingo on wheels!' squealed Anna with delight.

'You ain't seen nothing yet!' said Stella, her neck craning up over the carnival float's winged sides. 'She's got a fair few surprises locked away in here.'

'It's amazing!' said Anna proudly.

T. Bear followed the float, fully dressed up and with his drum strapped to his chest and drumsticks in his paws. Anna had never seen him so happy.

'This is our best carnival float ever,' he growled happily.

'Wait for me!' called Lemmy.

The lemur bounced through the revolving door, head to toe in brightly coloured feathers. He shook the maracas in both his paws.

'I wouldn't miss this for the world!' he said. 'Does it breathe fire?'

'On you get!' said Stella. 'And, no, it doesn't breathe fire. It does something much better than that.'

'What could be better than that?' asked Lemmy.

'You wait!'

Anna, Lemmy and the flamingos clambered up on to the float, and T. Bear took his place in front on the road.

'Here we go!' said Stella. 'Revvin' her up!'

The engine grew louder.

'Everyone ready?' asked Anna.

T. Bear banged
his drum, and they
headed off towards
the Opera House
and the start of the
parade.

The carnival
filled the whole of
Animal Boulevard.
A sea of animals of all kinds stretched
as far as the eye could see. The raucous
cheering was deafening. There were
floats and groups galore lined up for the
procession on the road. The local football
team was out in force, so too were a
troupe of fire-breathing goats, and a
huge dragon costume snaked through
the crowd.

'What a sight!' said Anna as they proudly took their place at the front of the parade.

'And there's Mr Ruffian's float,' said Lemmy, frowning. 'But where is he?'

Second in line, behind Hotel Flamingo's float, was the Glitz's effort, which was gold and furry and shaped like a leaping lion.

'I bet he's got something planned, darling,' said Ms Fragranti. 'But it will never be as wonderful as our display.'

Anna feared the worst. 'He always has something up his sleeve, doesn't he?' she said.

'Don't worry,' said Stella. 'You're going to like this.'

She switched on their sound system,

which was hidden inside the float's body, and Anna was amazed by how loud it was.

'Brilliant!' she cried. 'No one will be louder than us.'

Mrs Toadly shouted to Anna from the kerbside. 'Looking mighty fine!' she said.

'And no sign of the storm! Mr Ruffian was right.'

'Let's hope so!' said Anna, though in the distance she could see the building storm clouds edging closer.

'Right then, all the way to the Cat's Paw Arena!' said Mrs Toadly. 'Are we all set?'

Anna gave Stella the nod and she revved the engines.

'All set!' cried Anna.

16

Mr Ruffian's Roar

Mrs Toadly lifted the loudspeaker to her mouth. 'Three! Two! One!' she cried.

With the screech of a klaxon horn, the carnival began. Cheers rang out, sound systems kicked in and a disco beat drove the parade down Animal Boulevard. T. Bear drummed away, leading the procession like a merry piper, smiling at the crowds on the pavement.

Nothing could wipe the smile from his face.

The flamingo float trundled forward as its giant head swept left and right.

'This is amazing!' said Anna.

'You wait,' said Stella, pressing a button. 'Watch this, Lemmy!'

There was a gurgle and a pop, and suddenly a shower of glistening bubbles floated out from the giant flamingo's beak and drifted over the crowd.

'Bubbles!' cheered Lemmy. Everyone loved a bubble, and they weren't half as dangerous as fire.

'Flamingo! Flamingo!' chanted Anna and Ms Fragranti, dancing happily aboard the float. The crowds cheered back.

But then an ear-piercing ROAR erupted from behind them. It was enough to shock everyone into looking back. Anna watched as the Glitz's lion-shaped float shook and wobbled, growling and grumbling as a hatch opened on its top. A huge inflatable lion sprang out, growing larger all the while. It floated upwards, and eventually the rope ties keeping it attached to the float tightened and held it in place overhead.

Mr Ruffian walked out on to the float, gloating over his surprise. The lion's dazzling, sparkling suit sprinkled the crowds with flecks of light as his disco lights swirled and spun.

Anna and Hotel Flamingo's display was well and truly overshadowed. And then Mr Ruffian started throwing out sweets and preaching about how the Glitz was the best hotel in town. It was louder than anything coming from Hotel Flamingo's float.

'Turn the volume up!' said Anna.

'It's already pretty high,' said Stella.

'Louder!' said Anna.

Stella did as she was told, and for a brief second they drowned out Mr Ruffian's voice. And then the speakers popped and fell silent. Smoke drifted up from the flamingo float's exhaust.

'I tried to warn you,' said Stella with a sigh.

Anna heard Mr Ruffian roar with laughter behind her.

'Talk about embarrassing,' said Anna.

'Don't worry, darling!' exclaimed Ms Fragranti. 'We will wow everyone with our tropical dance!'

As they wound down Animal Boulevard the flamingo troupe flew on to the road and formed a triangle around T. Bear. And then with a swish of their wings their performance began. If any creature could draw attention to itself, it was Ms Fragranti.

Mr Ruffian's music grew louder still. The flamingos became more animated, pulling unusual shapes and twisting in spirals. But Ms Fragranti started to look worried. Her feathers ruffled.

'Miss Anna!' she cried. 'Look!'

Anna looked past the giant lion floating in the sky and saw the storm coming on fast. A huge black cloud was threatening to wreak havoc. The daylight started to fade. The breeze turned into a gale.

'I told you a storm was on its way!' Ms Fragranti said as a bruising wind whipped up and coursed along Animal Boulevard.

And here it comes! thought Anna, feeling the first spots of rain land on her face. 'Take cover!'

17

A Rough Time

As the heavens opened on Animal Boulevard every animal took cover wherever they could. Mrs Toadly raced through the growing storm to Anna.

'Oh, it's a mighty fine mess we're in!' she said, although being a toad she didn't mind the rain at all. 'Why was I not stronger with Mr Ruffian? There's too many people to get safely out of this weather!'

Suddenly Anna heard a terrible ripping noise. She turned to see the giant inflatable lion break from one of its ropes and whip backwards. It pulled Mr Ruffian's float into the crowds, crashing into the buildings that lined the boulevard.

Animals fled in all directions. It was chaos. *People will get hurt*, thought Anna. She had to think – and fast!

'T. Bear!' she shouted. 'Bang your drum as loud as you can!'

'Yes, miss!' he replied.

'We've got to lead everyone to safety!'
she said. 'To Hotel Flamingo!'

Lightning coursed down from the sky,
splitting a palm tree in two.

'Everyone?' said Mrs Toadly.

'Everyone!' said Anna, jumping from
the float. 'We've got plenty of space!
This way!'

The flamingo float cut through the
growing storm on its way to the hotel.
Led by Anna, T. Bear and the flamingos,
the crowds reached the hotel and

squeezed through the revolving doors.

Eva looked utterly shocked as hundreds of drenched animals descended upon them. Hilary worried about the mess they would make of the carpet. Mr and Mrs Kunkworth ran out of the way to hide, and Wilbur jumped to his feet.

'Can I help, miss?' he asked.

'Get everyone into the ballroom!' said Anna, directing the animals downstairs.

'We need to escape this storm!'

'Right you are!' he said.

Wilbur had spent lots of time in the ballroom over the previous few nights, listening to the band practise. He knew exactly what to do and where to go.

'Follow me!' he said, stomping down the beautiful staircase.

Anna marched straight to Eva. 'We need drinks, all of them,' she said.

'You got it,' said Eva.

'MADAME LE PIG!' shouted Anna.

'We need food! All of it!'

'What is this?!' squealed Madame Le Pig, raging from her kitchen. She quickly spotted the immense herd of animals and skidded to a halt. 'Oh my word! All the animals in the world are in our hotel!'

'And we need to feed them,' said Anna.

'I will do what I can,' said the chef.

'And me!' exclaimed Ms Fragranti. 'You know what I shall do? I shall entertain them!'

Anna smiled. In times of need everyone pulled together.

Mrs Toadly burst through the revolving door and brushed water off herself.

'That's it!' she cried. 'Everyone's out of it!'

'Everyone?' said Anna. 'Where's Mr Ruffian? I would have known if he'd come in.'

'I didn't see him,' said Mrs Toadly.

The storm was getting worse, and not even the hotel felt safe. Everything was rattling and shaking, from windowsills to guttering, and Anna watched as tiles smashed on to the ground outside the hotel. They were quickly followed by an uprooted palm tree skidding down the road.

'I know what you're thinking,' growled T. Bear. 'And I don't like it.'

'But this is a hurricane,' said Anna. 'No one should be outside in this, not even him.'

'Quite right,' said Mrs Toadly.

Lemmy and Stella appeared from the back of the lobby, having parked the flamingo float.

'Glad we're out of that!' said Lemmy.

'I have to go back out,' said Anna.

'You're mad,' said Stella. 'That wind could lift you off your feet.'

Suddenly the giant inflatable lion raced past the window and got caught on a lamp post. Trailing in its wake was Mr Ruffian, hanging on for dear life as the wind swirled him back and forth.

'We must hurry. Have we got any rope?' said Anna.

'You're kidding, aren't you?' said Lemmy.

'This is Hotel Flamingo,' said Anna with grim determination. 'Everyone is

welcome here. Even him. We have to do
all we can to save him.'

'Give me a minute,' said Stella, running
away. 'I'll be right back.'

Anna walked to the revolving door,
which was turning on its own in the wind.

Mr Ruffian roared loudly.

'Here! I'm here!' he cried, flipping up
and down in the wind.

Stella and T. Bear approached carrying
a long line of rope. Anna tied it about
herself and knotted it tight.

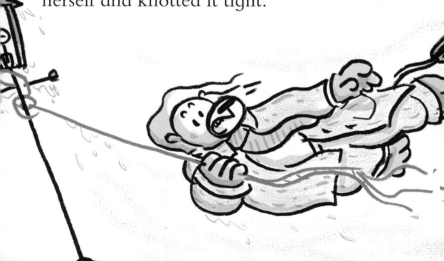

T. Bear took hold of the other end. 'I'll let you out slowly,' he said. 'Once you're within reach grab hold of him, and we'll reel you in.'

Anna nodded. She stepped out into the gale and felt the wind and rain hit her. Each step forward took her two steps sidewards. But she kept going.

'You've got it!' shouted T. Bear in encouragement.

The lamp post drew closer. Anna was about to reach out and grab the lion, when suddenly the lamp post buckled and Mr Ruffian flew a few metres backwards.

'Hurry, girl!' he said.

Anna bit her lip to stop her saying anything rude, and with two more steps forward she was able to grip on to Mr

Ruffian's dazzling jacket.

'Now!' she said, pulling him down to the ground.

Mr Ruffian took hold of her hand and dragged himself along the rope that stretched into Hotel Flamingo. T. Bear pulled them in just as the street lamp broke free of the ground and shot up into the sky, taking the giant inflatable lion with it.

18

The Show Must Go On

'Dude, that was cool!' said Suzi Suzi.

All the band had been woken by the raging storm and come down to the lobby to watch Anna's amazing feat. Anji Wax gave her a wide, beaming smile. Kool Bananas patted her on the back in amazement.

Mr Ruffian was exhausted, and his once immaculate hair hung unhappily over his face.

Eva passed him a hot drink and wrapped a blanket about his shoulders. 'Enjoy!' she said cheerfully.

'There is very little to enjoy about this,' he growled.

'At least you are safe,' said Anna.

'I suppose you deserve a thank-you,' he admitted.

Anna very nearly smiled.

'It was a wonderful thing you did there!' said Mrs Toadly. She pulled a Golden Palm statue from inside her jacket. 'I know it's not much, but I

think you deserve it after all this. It's just a shame the parade was such a washout.'

'You do realise the carnival is still raging downstairs, don't you?' said Lemmy, smiling.

'What's that?' said Anna.

They walked down into the ballroom, and a giant conga – led by Ms Fragranti – circled the hall. Mac and Lil Macaw and their parrot friends

danced along, cheering and whooping.

'You have the best hotel!' said Lil with a laugh, as she passed by.

'Those animals know how to party!' said Kool.

'It's a shame you didn't get to perform,' said Lemmy.

'No one will be performing in this weather,' said Anna. 'Those Sugar Bunnies won't have a single person to watch them.'

'They'll have Mr Sweet,' said Suzi with a smile.

Mrs Toadly surveyed the ballroom with her enormous smile back on her face. 'Just look around you,' she said. 'I would say this is a huge crowd to perform to!'

'Good grief, you're right!' said Anna.

'What say you-all? How about being the first act to play in the Hotel Flamingo ballroom?'

Suzi punched the air. 'Dude, you're on!'

19

The Ballroom Blitz

The band played all their greatest hits, watched by the whole of Animal Boulevard. All of Hotel Flamingo's guests and staff were present. Mr and Mrs Kunkworth bopped and jived, Lemmy pogoed up and down, and even Mrs Turpington joined in – although her moves were a little more graceful than Lemmy's. The ballroom was rocking and rolling, literally.

'I wonder if this is breaking health and safety rules?' asked T. Bear as the floor bounced up and down beneath him.

'No one will forget this gig or our hotel,' said Anna happily. 'And that's the most important thing. Something good will come out of this day!'

As the band finished, after three encores at Lemmy's insistence, the party threatened to get going once more. The storm had finally passed, and as word got down to the ballroom that the outside was safe once more, Mac Macaw attempted to reboot the conga.

'Miss,' asked T. Bear, 'I know this has been fun, but we

really should ask everyone to leave now.'

'I think you're right,' said Anna.

She walked over to the band and took the microphone from Suzi Suzi. 'Thank you for coming!' she said, her words echoing around the ballroom. 'But now the storm's over, if you'd please take your things and leave quietly so as not to disturb our guests . . .'

'We *are* your guests!' cheered the parrots, and they started dancing again, as did everyone else.

Anna tried speaking but her words were drowned out by the stomping. 'Can we turn it up more?' Anna asked the band.

'Sure, dude,' said Suzi, turning up the speaker. 'Let's kick it up to the max!'

Anna raised the microphone to her mouth. 'This concert is –'

A deafening POP blew out of the speaker and a wisp of smoke lifted into the air.

The revellers were stunned into silence. Then Anna noticed Mr and Mrs Kunkworth scurrying away up the staircase to the lobby. Anna had an inkling of what was about to happen. Despite her ears hurting, she smiled.

A foul stench filled the room and it emptied faster than the sea after a shark sighting.

'That's one way to do it, miss,' said T. Bear, holding his nose.

Anna watched over the lobby that night
as The Nocturnal Animals readied to
leave. She was surprised to see Wilbur
helping them gather their equipment.

'Hello, Wilbur,' she said happily.

'Evening, miss,' he said. 'You'll never
guess what?'

'What?'

'I've got myself a job,' said Wilbur.
'Seems like I'm one of the band now.'

'You are?' said Anna. 'That's brilliant.'

'It's just like what I did in the army,' he said. 'I can carry their gear and get them to gigs and stuff. All thanks to you giving me a chance.'

'That's Hotel Flamingo for you,' said Anna, smiling.

'It is, miss,' he said.

'Dude, this is the coolest hotel in the world,' said Suzi as she appeared alongside Lemmy with a marker pen in her hand.

Anna noticed that the band had autographed Lemmy's long tail.

'I'm never washing it off!' he said, all starry-eyed.

Kool Bananas sloped into the lobby and drummed along the front desk before dinging the bell with a flourish. He twirled his sticks before landing them in T. Bear's paws.

'This place rocks,' he said. 'Keep the beat alive, bear.'

'These are for me?' said T. Bear as the bushbaby wandered off.

The drumsticks were too small for a bear's paws, but they were the best present

T. Bear had ever been given.

'You bet,' said Kool. 'Never stop
banging that drum.'

'I won't,' said
T. Bear.

Anji Wax ran to Anna and hugged
her so tightly that she thought her head
might pop.

'Love this place,' said Anji tearfully.

'You do?' said Anna
with surprise.

'Wombats are
supposed to fear
nothing,' said Anji,
'but Mr Sweet –
I didn't like him.'

The wombat's grip
was making it hard for

Anna to breathe. 'He wasn't very nice,' croaked Anna.

'But seeing you stand up to him . . .' said Anji, 'it taught me a lot. I'll never forget this place.'

Anji's paws loosened round Anna. She squeezed Anna's hand one last time and headed to the door.

Once the band and Wilbur had driven off into the night, Anna couldn't believe how quiet it was, nor how tired she was.

'Same again next year?' said Lemmy.

Anna sat down in a chair and slumped backwards. 'You bet,' she said, smiling.

A NOTE FROM THE AUTHOR

Writing a story about an animal hotel is a dream come true for me. I love learning about animals (my favourites are lemurs!) and I love drawing them, but I particularly love customer service.

So, as much as I'd like to stay at Hotel Flamingo and eat Madame Le Pig's amazing food, I would actually really like to work there. Yes, you heard right. Tidying the place up, planning and cooking meals, booking shows, making people happy . . . oh, that would be better than anything!

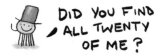

DID YOU FIND
ALL TWENTY
OF ME?